Tracy Brown

ILLUSTRATIONS BY
Paula Wegman

Kalaniot Books
Moosic, Pennsylvania

It was so unfair!

Sarah had been practicing her ballet routine for months. Now she was going to have to miss performing her solo because her cousin Lizzy's wedding was on the exact same day.

She had worked so hard to prepare—staying late after dance class and even missing her best friend's birthday party to rehearse with her troupe.

Sarah knew every move of her routine by heart. As she practiced, the delicate sounds of the violin filled her head, and she let the music guide her. And as she danced, Sarah became lost in another world.

First Position

Second Position

Third Position

Fourth Position

Fifth Position

Finally, she held the skirts of her poufy crinoline dress, bringing her left leg behind her right, bending low, and bowing her head—the perfect curtsy.

On the day of Lizzy's wedding, Sarah looked
at her recital dress sparkling in the closet.

"Sarah, we need to leave. Please put on your dress," Sarah's mother yelled up the stairs.

"I'm ready!"
announced Sarah.

"There's no time to change," said her father. "Let's just go."

Sarah fidgeted in her seat during the wedding ceremony until the cantor began to sing. The song sounded soft and sweet, like the lullabies her mother used to sing to her. Sarah felt goosebumps on her arms.

Seven times Sarah counted Lizzy circling around Ben, the groom, her pearly gown trailing behind her. It was like a dance!

Smash! Ben stomped on a glass, and the wedding ceremony
was over. Everyone shouted, "Mazel tov!"

The guests filed into the reception hall, and the band began to play a slow, quiet tune. All around Sarah, everyone hurried to join hands. As the music's rhythm began to pick up speed, so did the steps of the dancers, circling the bride and groom.

Sarah's mother and father rushed to join in, too.

"What are you doing?" asked Sarah as her mother tried to pull her onto the dance floor.

"The band is playing 'Hava Nagila.' We're joining the hora," her mother said.

When Sarah wrinkled her brow, her father explained, "It's the traditional Jewish celebration dance.

"Mommy and I danced the hora at our wedding. And we will dance the hora at your bat mitzvah."

"C'mon," said her mother, "you love to dance!" But Sarah shook her head.

This dance wasn't nearly as graceful as her elegant ballet routine.

Sarah watched as her parents and the other guests twirled about in a circle. It looked like so much fun. Sarah couldn't help but tap her toes to the catchy beat.

open

Cross

Hand in hand, the dancers moved to the right, their left foot behind right—a kick to the left, a kick to the right.

Over and over, the steps continued until the dancers switched directions.

When the guests stopped dancing and lifted Lizzy and Ben high in the air on chairs, Sarah leaned closer to the circle, feeling the excitement of the guests.

As Lizzy's chair was lowered back to the floor, she looked right at Sarah. She reached out her hand and pulled Sarah into the center of the dance circle.

Hava Neranenah, hava neranenah,

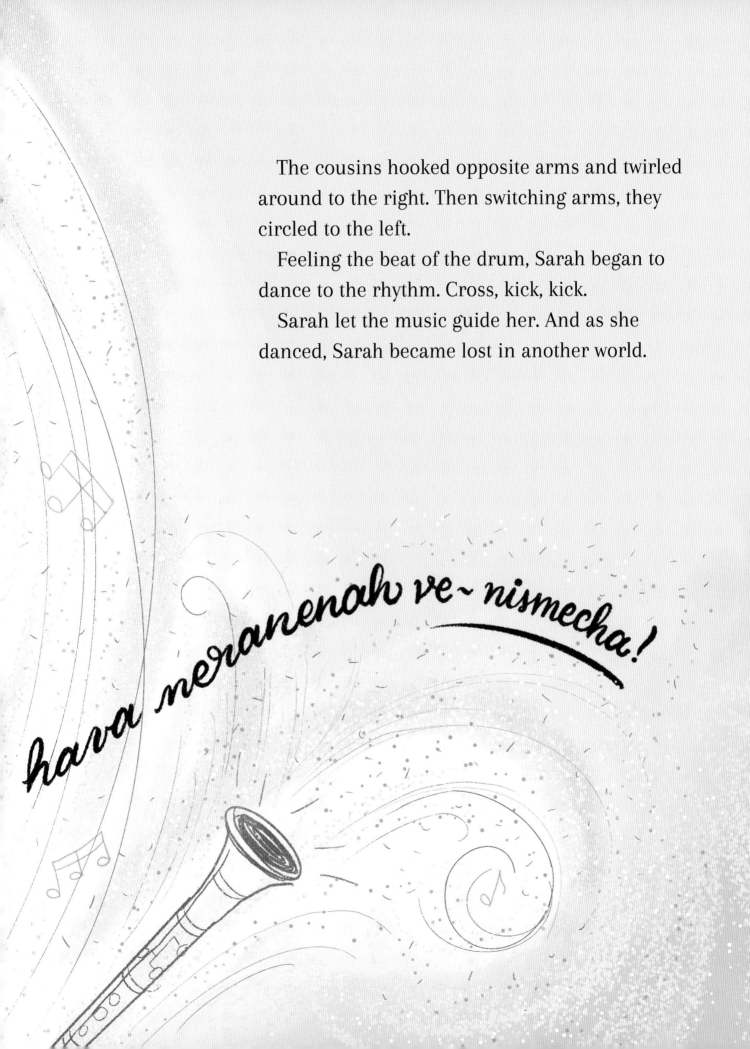

The cousins hooked opposite arms and twirled around to the right. Then switching arms, they circled to the left.

Feeling the beat of the drum, Sarah began to dance to the rhythm. Cross, kick, kick.

Sarah let the music guide her. And as she danced, Sarah became lost in another world.

hava neranenah ve~ nismecha!

When she finally began to slow down, Sarah found herself alone in the center of the circle, the wedding guests surrounding her, clapping. They were clapping for her.

She had danced her solo after all!

Sarah held the skirts of her poufy
crinoline dress, bringing her left leg
behind her right, bending low, and
bowing her head—the perfect curtsy.

Jewish Wedding Traditions

AUFRUF: A ceremony at the synagogue observed by some couples on a Shabbat prior to the wedding, where they receive a special blessing.

KETUBAH: Before the wedding ceremony, the couple signs a *ketubah*, a Jewish marriage contract. The *ketubah* outlines their rights and responsibilities to one another.

BEDEKEN: A tradition where the groom covers the bride with a veil prior to the wedding ceremony. Some believe that this is a symbol of Rebecca's modesty during her first meeting with Issac.

CHUPPAH: Lizzy and Ben were married under a *chuppah,* or wedding canopy. To some the *chuppah* represents the Jewish home the couple will build together. The *chuppah* is open on all sides, signifying that family and guests will always be welcome, just as Abraham and Sarah always welcomed guests inside their tent.

CIRCLING (*HAKAFOT*): Lizzy circles clockwise around Ben seven times, symbolizing the creation of a new family circle. In some cases, couples choose to circle each other three times, adding one final circle together.

EXCHANGING RINGS: During the wedding ceremony, the couple place a perfectly round ring on each other's index finger and recite the marriage blessing. It is customary that the ring is plain, with no stones or gems, and also round and unbroken, just as the love between the couple is everlasting and unbroken.

BREAKING THE GLASS: At the end of the wedding ceremony, Ben smashes a glass and the guests yell *mazel tov* (congratulations). The glass represents the destruction of the Temple in Jerusalem.

THE HORA: Lizzy and Ben and their guests dance the hora, an energetic circle dance. During the hora, it is traditional for the couple to be lifted on chairs while the wedding guests dance in a circle around them.

KLEZMER MUSIC: Originated with European Jews in the eighteenth century and was often played during celebrations. The tune "Hava Nagila" ("Come Let Us Rejoice") is a favorite of klezmer bands.

*To my rock, Larry, and to Katie, Annie, Sammy—and his bride Megan—
for all of the "solos" missed doing the right thing.* —T. B.

To my family, thank you for telling me our history and for teaching me how to draw my own. —P. W.

Text copyright © 2021 by Tracy Brown. Illustrations by Paula Wegman copyright © 2021 Endless Mountains Publishing Company | Published by Kalaniot Books, an imprint of Endless Mountains Publishing Company | 72 Glenmaura National Boulevard, Suite 104B, Moosic, Pennsylvania 18570 | www.KalaniotBooks.com | All rights reserved. International copyright secured. No part of this book may be reproduced, stored in a retrieval system, or transmitted in any form or by any means—electronic, mechanical, photocopying, recording, or otherwise—without the prior written permission of Endless Mountains Publishing Company, except for the inclusion of brief quotations in an acknowledged review. Library of Congress Control Number: 2020944211 | ISBN: 978-1-7350875-0-4 | First Printing.